W9-AFD-826

GRANDFATHER'S CHRISTMAS CAMP

BETA E. KING LIBRARY

GRANDFATHER'S CHRISTMAS CAMP

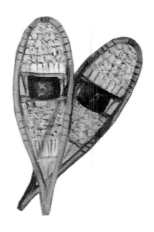

BY **MARC McCUTCHEON**

ILLUSTRATED BY **KATE KIESLER**

CLARION BOOKS/NEW YORK

RETA E. KING LIBRARY
CHADRON STATE COLLEGE
CHADRON, NE 69337

Clarion Books
a Houghton Mifflin Company imprint
215 Park Avenue South, New York, NY 10003
Text copyright © 1995 by Marc McCutcheon
Illustrations copyright © 1995 by Kate Kiesler

The illustrations for this book were executed in oils on Bristol paper.
The text was set in 16/20-point Goudy.

All rights reserved.

For information about permission to reproduce selections from this book, write to
Permissions, Houghton Mifflin Company,
215 Park Avenue South, New York, NY 10003.

For information about this and other Houghton Mifflin trade and reference books
and multimedia products, visit The Bookstore at Houghton Mifflin
on the World Wide Web at (http://www.hmco.com/trade/).

Printed in the USA.

Library of Congress Cataloging-in-Publication Data

McCutcheon, Marc.
Grandfather's Christmas camp / by Marc McCutcheon ; illustrated by Kate Kiesler.
p.   cm.
Summary: when Grandfather's three-legged dog Mr. Biggins disappears
on Christmas Eve, Lizzie and Grandfather go up the mountain
to find him and have an unusual adventure.
ISBN 0-395-69626-7   PA ISBN 0-395-86629-4
[1. Christmas—Fiction. 2. Grandfathers—Fiction. 3. Dogs—Fiction.]
I. Kiesler, Kate A., ill. II. Title.
PZ7.M4784165Gr 1995
[E—dc20]   94-15589
CIP
AC

HOR 10 9 8 7 6 5 4

To Kara and Macky

—M.M.

For Pa 'Dette,
who has always known the lure of the woods

—K.K.

GRANDFATHER AND I can't find Mr. Biggins.

We whistle for him out back. We shout for him in the meadow. Grandfather blows his alpenhorn. But Mr. Biggins doesn't come.

"Gone up the mountain after deer again," Grandfather grumbles. "I'll have to go fetch the old three-legged fool. He'll never make it back with this snow comin'."

"I want to go, Grandfather."

"On Christmas Eve?" His eyes blaze at me. For a long time he sizes me up, then growls, "Want you dressed from head to toenail, Lizzie. And I don't want you bellyaching or holding me up." Grandfather is big and leathery, and he doesn't like slowpokes. He's a mountain man.

I pull on three pairs of socks, long underwear, thick pants, boots,
undershirt, shirt, sweatshirt, sweater, coat, hat, scarf, and mittens.

Grandfather packs a backpack "just in case."

We clomp in our snowshoes through the old-growth forest. Then up one
hill, then another, steeper, steeper. Pretty soon my legs feel like logs.

"Mr. Biggins!" Grandfather shouts.

"Mr. Biggins!" I shout.

"Mr. Biggins!" the mountain echoes back.

The snow swirls down in a carousel of sugar and doilies. Icicles hang from the trees like glass ornaments. My breath smokes. Puff, puff, puff.

A buck leaps across the trail.

A raccoon dumps snow on us from the top of a fir tree.

Grandfather yanks off his mittens, jams his fingers in his mouth, and whistles so loud for Mr. Biggins that I have to hold my ears.

He grouches at me. "Pick up the pace, child. You can't walk like a baby up a mountain."

We go up the zigzagging trail Grandfather calls a switchback. It's easier to climb than a straight path. But my feet are tired anyway.

"Mr. Biggins!" Grandfather roars into the wilderness. "You're a contemptible mongrel to be pulling this on Christmas Eve! I've a mind to leave you to your own devices!"

But I know Grandfather doesn't mean it. He loves Biggins too much.

We climb. Higher, higher, to the clouds. The trees grow smaller, smaller, their branches twisted into strange shapes. Grandfather calls this place the Alpine Zone.

I yell for Biggins but the wind swallows up my voice. I can't holler as loud as Grandfather.

We sit down in a clearing and share a candy bar from the backpack. Grandfather rakes snow out of his beard with his fingers. He stoops to examine some footprints going up the trail. "Those are Biggins' pawprints, all right. No mistaking a three-legged dog."

I begin to shiver but I don't dare tell Grandfather. I clamp my mouth tight so my teeth won't chatter. I wish I had a bigger coat.

"Hoooooooooooooo . . ." an owl hoots from some rotten tree hole.

"Last trail marker," Grandfather says near the top of the mountain. "Can't go much farther."

We climb over a high mound, past the fire tower. Grandfather turns around and looks at me. "Legs tired?"

"Nope," I lie.

"We'll make camp. Cook some meat. Biggins'll smell it and come running. Then I'll give him a piece of my mind."

"Okay, Grandfather."

We gather wood, make a fire. It's hard to start a fire up here, Grandfather says, because the air is thin. But he can always get a fire going, even when it's raining.

Grandfather cups his hands around his mouth and takes a giant breath. "MR. BIGGINS! HERE, DOG! SUPPER, DOG!"

But Mr. Biggins doesn't come.

Grandfather empties his pack. He fries venison and melts cheese on it. He makes a hot sandwich and hands it to me. Then we crush saltines into our steaming cocoa.

The meat smell drifts all over the mountain. But Mr. Biggins doesn't come.

The snow stops drifting down and the clouds clear. Suddenly stars twinkle from a million places. The sky is a tall one tonight, Grandfather says.

"Orion!" he shouts, as he points at a giant in the sky. "And that bright red star . . . Betelgeuse! That blue one . . . Rigel! I can name 'em all."

A curtain of rosy light from the Aurora flickers across heaven. "Red carpet for St. Nick, that," he says. "Mr. Biggins!"

RETA E. KING LIBRARY

We clean up our supper. Then Grandfather looks at me hard. "Can't leave without Biggins, you know. We'll have to bivouac. That okay by you?"
I look around at the deep snow. It's too deep for Biggins to run very far in. "He can't make it home by himself," I say. "Christmas can wait, Grandfather."
Grandfather looks at me and then he nods.

"And it wouldn't be Christmas without Biggins, anyway," I say.
Grandfather smiles at me.

He gathers snow in a pile. I help pile on more and more snow. Then we
hollow out an igloo. "It's not a hotel," Grandfather says, "but it'll keep us
warm till morning."

I curl up next to Grandfather. He feels warm, and he smells like woodsmoke and spice. I hear him whisper something about Mr. Biggins. Then he snores.

Lying in the dark, I miss Biggins' claws going *ticka, ticka, ticka* across the floor. I listen for barks and panting. I smell the air for stinky fur and breath. But there is only the dark.

In the middle of the night I dream of bells. Jingling. Jangling. Echoing across the sky.

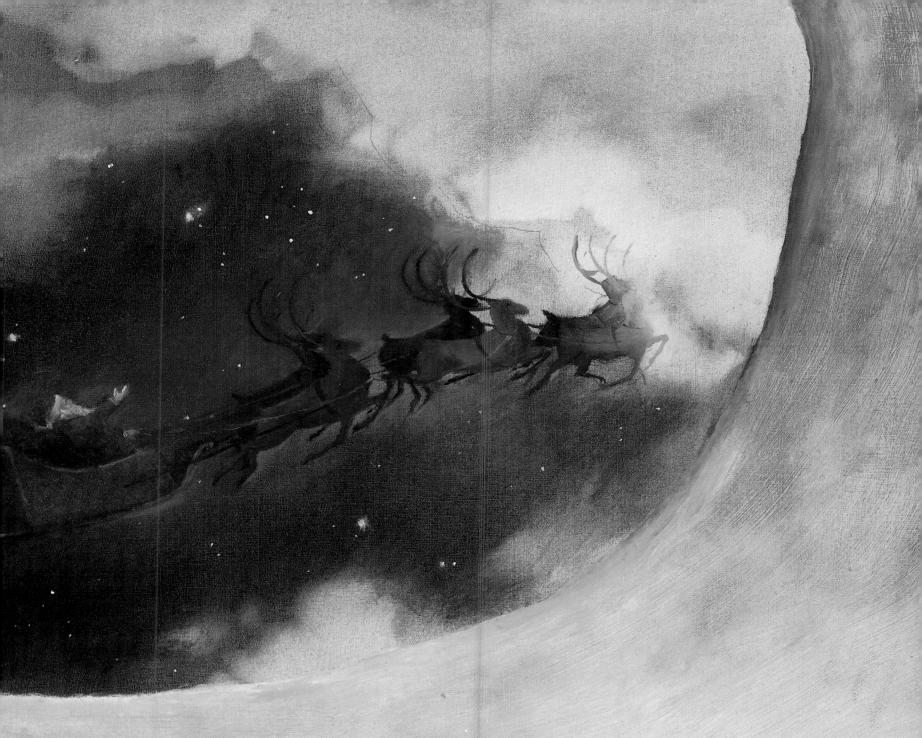

I squint up through the roof of the igloo at the stars and see it. The sleigh, the long train of reindeer, and St. Nick. Passing over the mountain. Then disappearing into a cloud.

I'm dreaming, I think, and curl up closer against Grandfather. Merry Christmas, Grandfather, I say in my sleep.

I wake to the smell of bacon frying in a pan. A three-legged brown missile with a jangling collar leaps on me and laps my nose. "Mr. Biggins!"

"Lost his way and didn't catch the doe . . . been eatin' like a starved pig," Grandfather says. "Come out, St. Nick brought you something."

"What is it?"

"Our ride home."

I see two runners lashed onto a long plank, a whittling knife in Grandfather's hands, a pile of wood shavings by his feet. He gives me a wink.

A sled.

We finish eating and pack up our mess. Grandfather gets on the sled in back. I get in front. Mr. Biggins squats in the middle and slobbers down my neck.

Whooooooooooooooooooosh . . .

Down the mountain trail, past the fire tower, around the gnarly trees, zigzag across the switchback, up over the humpbacks and shoulders, *bump, bump, bump* over the moguls, around and down a chute, *sssssssshhhhhhhhhhhhhhh* past the frozen pond, through the old-growth forest, *galumpabump* over the washboard foothills and through the meadow to the old log cabin with the swaybacked roof.

Me, Grandfather, and Mr. Biggins, safe and home on Christmas Day.